Dear Parent:
Your child's love of reading starts here!

I Can Read Books have introduced children to the joy of reading since 1957. Featuring award-winning authors and illustrators and a fabulous cast of beloved characters, I Can Read Books set the standard for beginning readers. From books your child reads with you to the first books they read alone, there are I Can Read Books for every stage of reading:

SHARED READING
Basic language, word repetition, and whimsical illustrations, ideal for sharing with your emergent reader

BEGINNING READING
Short sentences, familiar words, and simple concepts for children eager to read on their own

READING WITH HELP
Engaging stories, longer sentences, and language play for developing readers

READING ALONE
Complex plots, challenging vocabulary, and high-interest topics for the independent reader

ADVANCED READING
Short paragraphs, chapters, and exciting themes for the perfect bridge to chapter books

Every child learns in a different way and at their own speed. Some read through each level in order. Others go back and forth between levels and read favorite books again and again. You can help your young reader improve and become more confident by encouraging their own interests and abilities.

A lifetime of discovery begins with the magical words, "I Can Read!"

HarperCollins®, ▄®, and I Can Read Book®
are trademarks of HarperCollins Publishers Inc.

The Berenstain Bears and the Baby Chipmunk
For information address HarperCollins Children's Books,
a division of HarperCollins Publishers,
195 Broadway, New York, NY 10007.
www.harperchildrens.com

Library of Congress Cataloging-in-Publication Data
Berenstain, Stan.
      The Berenstain Bears and the baby chipmunk / Stan & Jan Berenstain.—1st ed.
          p.   cm.— (An I can read book)
      Summary: When Sister finds a baby chipmunk in the yard, the Bear family cares for it in
their home until it lets them know that it is no longer a baby.
      ISBN 0-06-058413-0 (pbk.)—ISBN 0-06-058412-2
      [1. Bears—Fiction. 2. Chipmunks—Fiction. 3. Babies—Fiction.] I. Berenstain, Jan. II. Title.
III. Series.
PZ7.B4483Beat 2005
[E]—dc21   2004019049
                                                                                                            CIP
                                                                                                            AC

Typography by Scott Richards

16 SCP 10 9 8 7 6
❖
First Edition

An I Can Read Book™

The Berenstain Bears
and the
Baby Chipmunk

Stan & Jan Berenstain

HarperCollins*Publishers*

It was a lovely day
in Bear Country.
The Bear family was enjoying
the sunshine.
Papa was resting.
Mama was working
in the garden.

Honey Bear was watching Mama.

Brother and Sister were

playing catch.

5

"Look!" said Sister. "A mouse!"

"That is not a mouse," said Brother.

"If it is not a mouse,

what is it?" asked Sister.

"It is a chipmunk," said Mama.

"A *baby* chipmunk."

"May we keep him, Mama?" cried Sister.

"May we? May we?"

"Look," said Brother.

"His eyes are not open yet."

"That's right," said Mama.

"This baby should be with his mother.

But she will not come if she sees us.

Come. We will hide behind the tree house.

Maybe she will come."

The Bears watched and watched.

But the mother chipmunk did not come.

"Now may we keep him?" cried Sister.

"May we? May we?"

"I think we shall have to," said Mama.

"At least for a while."

"That is right," said Papa.

"Babies need to be fed and kept warm."

"Papa, do you have a clean hanky?"
asked Mama.

Mama picked up the baby chipmunk
and tucked him into Papa's hanky.

Then they took the baby chipmunk
into the house.

13

"Sister," said Mama. "Please get one of your doll's baby bottles. Brother, please get some milk and honey."

The baby chipmunk was very hungry.
As he drank from the bottle,
he opened his eyes.
They were big and brown.

"Let's name him Brown Eyes," said Sister.

"That is as good a name as any," said Mama.

Papa got a box for a bed.

Brother made it cozy.

Brown Eyes liked his new bed.

Baby Honey liked to watch him.

Soon Brown Eyes was fast asleep.

The next morning,
Sister and Brother
woke up early.
They ran downstairs
to see Brown Eyes.
The box was there.
But he was not.
They looked all around.

"There he is!" said Brother.

Brown Eyes was up on the table.

He had knocked over the sugar bowl.

He was eating sugar.

"I guess he needs more

than milk and honey," said Sister.

The cubs went outside.

They got some seeds.

Brown Eyes was very small.

But he had big, chipmunk teeth.

Just like that, the seeds were gone.

Brown Eyes loved to play.

What he loved to do most

was explore.

He explored Mama's vegetable bin.

OH, DEAR!

He explored Papa's desk.

OH, NO!

He explored Mama's sewing basket.

OH, MY!

Then one day,

he explored one place too many.

He explored Papa's pant leg—

all the way up to the knee!

While he was up there,

he tried out his big, sharp teeth.

"You know what I think?" asked Mama.

"I think Brown Eyes is telling us something.

He is telling us he is ready

to go out in the world.

He is ready to join his friends."

"But, Mama!" said Sister.

"I don't want him to go! I love him so!"

"We all love him," said Mama.

"But it is not fair to make him a pet.

Chipmunks need to be free.

They need to explore."

"There are not many good places
to explore inside."
The cubs thought about:
Mama's vegetable bin,

Papa's desk,

Mama's sewing basket,

and Papa's pant leg.

"Outside," said Mama, "Brown Eyes

will be able to explore all of nature."

As usual, Mama was right.

The Bear family didn't even

have to say good-bye.

They saw him every day
playing with his friends
and exploring nature—
right in their own backyard.